The really, really, really big dinosaur

Richard Byrne

'One for him and one for me.

One for him and one for me.'

Finlay was sharing out jelly beans
to have with his friend when . . .

a **big dinosaur** walked past.

'Would you like a jelly bean?'
asked Finlay.

'I want them all!'
said the big (and rather rude) dinosaur.

'Oh, I couldn't give them
all to you,' said Finlay,
'you see, they belong
to my friend.'

'Well tell your little friend, wherever he is, that I want **his jelly beans!**'

'He's asleep,' said Finlay.
'But he's a really, really, really big friend.'

'Oh, I'm really, **really**, **really** scared!'
said the big (and rather cheeky) dinosaur.
'Everyone knows I'm the
biggest and **strongest**
dinosaur around here!
Just w-a-i-t and . . .

'You're making that up,' said the big dinosaur. 'Anyway, I'm definitely the best at jumping

'Well I'd like to see your pretend friend

lift anything as **high** as this!'
said the big dinosaur.

'He could do that in his sleep,' said Finlay.

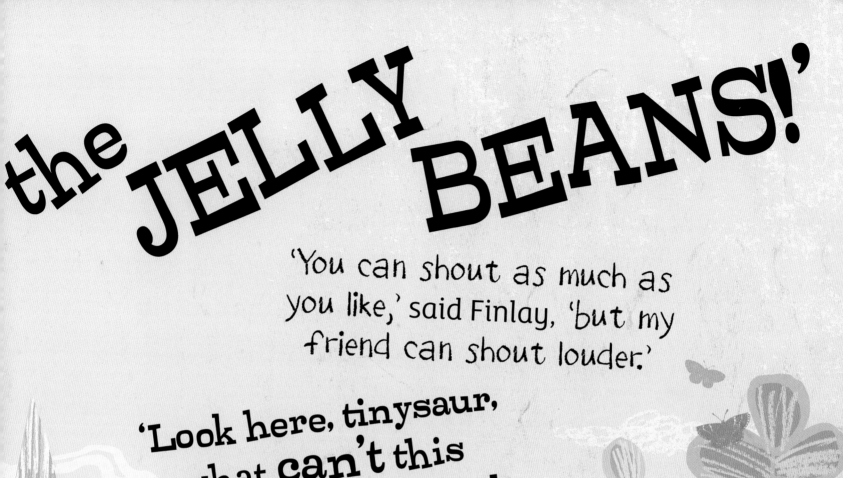

the JELLY BEANS!'

'You can shout as much as you like,' said Finlay, 'but my friend can shout louder.'

'Look here, tinysaur, what **can't** this make-believe friend of yours do?'

Finlay thought for a moment.

'Oh, yes. He's
afraid of dark,
scary places so
he would never go
into that cave
on his own . . .'

Just then, the big dinosaur grabbed
the jar of jelly beans and ran into the cave.

Finlay giggled. 'Don't worry, he **could** eat you but he **won't!**'

'**JELLY BEANS AND TREETOPS ARE MY FAVOURITES!**'

said the really, really, really big (and rather friendly) dinosaur.

'First one to the bottom wins the jelly beans!' said Finlay playfully.

Everyone knew that the big dinosaur was the best at S-l-i-d-i-n-g.

But this time . . .

he was happy just sharing.

'One for him **and** one for you **and** one for me. One for him …'

'and one for you …'

For Stella, Ellis, Harley, Archie, Kim, Mia and Ella.
And a really, really, really big thank you to Helen and Karen.

OXFORD
UNIVERSITY PRESS

Great Clarendon Street, Oxford OX2 6DP

Oxford University Press is a department of the University of Oxford.
It furthers the University's objective of excellence in research,
scholarship, and education by publishing worldwide in

Oxford   New York

Auckland Cape Town Dar es Salaam Hong Kong Karachi
Kuala Lumpur Madrid Melbourne Mexico City Nairobi
New Delhi Shanghai Taipei Toronto

With offices in
Argentina Austria Brazil Chile Czech Republic France Greece
Guatemala Hungary Italy Japan Poland Portugal Singapore
South Korea Switzerland Thailand Turkey Ukraine Vietnam

Oxford is a registered trade mark of Oxford University Press
in the UK and in certain other countries

Text and illustrations © Richard Byrne 2012

The moral rights of the author/illustrator have been asserted
Database right Oxford University Press (maker)

First published in 2012

British Library Cataloguing in Publication Data
Data available

ISBN: 978-0-19-275763-0 (hardback)
ISBN: 978-0-19-275764-7 (paperback)

10 9 8 7 6 5 4 3 2 1

Printed in China

Paper used in the production of this book is a natural,
recyclable product made from wood grown in sustainable forests.
The manufacturing process conforms to the environmental
regulations of the country of origin.